Rain Minnows [Notecards and Poems]

Copyright © 2020 Joshua Bridgwater Hamilton

Published by Gnashing Teeth Publishing. All rights reserved.

Original Cover Art by Leticia Bajuyo

The font used is Verdana for ease of reading for those with dyslexia.

Editor-in-Chief Karen Cline-Tardiff

Copy Editor Jennifer Taylor

Printed in the United States of America

ISBN 978-1-7340495-4-1

Fiction: Poetry

Table of Contents

Rain Minnows
[Notecards and Poems]

[R]ain Minnows-I

Pine Rustled Sheets
Char Tussled Wind

[B]irthday Note: Notecard #29

Earth breathes you
Fills you taut the circumference
Of sound, arpeggio'd such
Thrumming sails till rips
Trebley tattered.
But take now pressure, vibe, rhythm,
And enchant this you-song
Into air, into lung
We breathe.

[F]ragmento: Madrugada enlazada

Lázaro alegre,
yo,
mojado todavía
de sombras y pereza
—Ángel González

Blood back
into fingers, the other
forearm draped—
crook of el-
bow over forehead
stealing morning
light from menace
of time, my passing
mitigated by the mint
of brushed teeth
exhale cool
canopy over pillow
breath into breath

[E]volution of the Lunger

Esta tormenta
huddles its tortoise shell
over the shocked birth — un pez,
a floodsy gripe, un grito, then ponderous
ponderosa bass fills the looming (sangre en el
templo).
Suspira...
             because it's back again,
mouth gaping — boca grande —
suffering oxygen instead of pure water.
Agua, Acqua, Aquatic —
the fish swimmer lives
between clear current
and mirror sky:
el cielo, la corriente, pasos pesados
llenando sin hueco.

[V]anity — Patina with Arrangement: Notecard #17

Mirrored double-agent indemnity
Will washed heretofore to wayward station
1.) On guard profile, a vestment memory
[Read-only as long as framed stencil
Curves curvature of flesh into carved relief]
2.) Identity's late arrival, latent in schedule
RAMmed, glimmery, full moment cast into
Dispersion —
Nostalgia in foyer, framed image staring,
An empire of furnitures, ottomans, this moon's
Settings

[T]ryst: Flirted, Fled

leaving no leavings
to find her trail again. Johnny
turned his coat collar against the cold,
painstakingly
folded warm penumbra away
from wind-chill thoughts.
Bells, flags, hulls lapped
at the moon surge in Winter Harbor.
Husbanded
to exotic rhythms, he knew
the hold settled in the quick water,
and he lurched forward
toward the slip.

[W]reckage of the Bright Remains: Notecard
#25

Lava land of touchscreens and action figures
Sinks memory's charred bedrock and floods on
Through the zen slap of unshared reality.
Out of bright remains dishwater,
                          wood crates,
                                    jam jars,
Where Grandma's Baptist ghost sparks out
Along the wire
Lighting up plug-ins,
                     frozen preservatives,
                               candidates.

[A]ugust Fare: Notecard #19

This guy, Johnny,
Sums his life up — elephant
Ears and hidden snipers —
Cotton candied pink in play and death,
After duck duck *ping*! on the midway
Comes times two the jungle-green lumen,
Toy-train clatter wooden at the mystic summit
Where staccato moons
                    pierce through a straight fair,
Fatten in memory grease,
                    wisdom the undergrowth.

[H]ymn to the Nails

Last column totaled
Surprised the numbers—
vertical nails in ink or light
framing the journey
through sedentary life,
recumbent death—
makes you want
to push fingers
into wild assumptions,
ignore yard and planters,
let vines grow hangdog
from cheeks, neck, hang doubt
one step out of coffee
and the morning tears its cushion
lays down nailed frame
on trellis to guide the green
of penetration. Thus, the dis -
quiet of time looks
to the senses, will
thereupon rip and exile
what shelter
was keeping.

9

[S]hadows of Architecture

Acaso todo esto sucederá sin ti
Pero junto a ti es más dichoso
—*José María Álvarez*

I let my body
and it contemplates me —
fervor, lightning, a warm
winter pavement
soaks my companion
to the eyetooth
(we out you let this help
no building forward destruction
good code
sinks trimmed lunar bed nail
beside my 6 a.m.
bride my temple)

let body live and some
elsewhere one takes me
palm pressed to the quick
and forethought rubs
her head un-
dermine and my temple un-
divided.

10

[W]inter Concrastination: Notecard #26

My grandiose plan has popped,
Settled the dreamy confetti
Into pocket lint. I saw it mount
A potent icebox, cool agendas
Descended from the ceiling —
Drywall half-life dusty crumbles.
Empty chapstick drums keep rhythm
While my lips gently shred
The hidden life of blood.

[R]ain Minnows-II

Crescent Tips Finger
Tap Warming Sink

[D]ebtor at Morning

Iron-smelted air
beyond the cracked window
thickens megaphone rattle of morning —
against this thin trickle of neck,
starvation burnished warm,
                        red-pressed tongue —
you, my friend.
But who's barbaric here?
Who the wise cutting down the middle thorax,
bleats of night departure —
who the task of day, its chest cracked wide
my foolish pinned to crumpled sheets,
fool dissecting limb of lamb,
or they that there expect
the daily
libation
feet strapped up,
veins poured
open.

[S]pill: Notecard #8

Time-stacked containers, wet sloshing contents
Saucerpanned across pavement — drunk
And ruffy, the stacked horizon tries
Repeatedly to twilight, but falters into noon.
We go hop, skip, & jump into party lights,
Corset woven into bare chest skin
And giving tattoo a gleaming gum-smack;
Phrases thread out precious perforations
Cinch bloodlet tapestry —
                              them slaked amnesias.

[P]oker Dead Mailer

Four men hunched
into the edges of a rickety
soap-box rectangle,
desperate ciphers of fate
concentrated onto one
simple table.
Jason wants a hit.
Soldier to the sinister
reaches a card through grimy smoke —
edge reaping hope
into tattered contrails, heavy
hung in the ship's hold.
Out. As Jason leans back,
murky prospects thicken air,
the table clutters —
divinely blin-
ded.

[D]ream Song for Humbert Humbert:
Sentimental Bicycle

Sore Johnny enters bar the Gran Vía entrance—
spectacular study of mute commute,
throws eyes wide open and beseeches blankly:

"Listen, fellow drinkers, listen country!
To the intimate bicycle wheel
bespoke a fiery pit of guilt
below the squeaking pleat of knicker,
listen summer crimes of violence
to weeping sensibility —
these rounded physics,
jouncing calisthenics
are our greatest,
grandest achievement.
(Achou!) (¡Salud!)"

Johnny, 50, penitent
in good old Mexico,
turning to the bar,
he believes in cycles,
turning chance to do things over,
the nothing he has done, turning

16

for tequila, for the rum,
for the gaze eternally returning
upon itself himself,
("Sí, ponme una — lo de siempre").

An anguish tread untreading,
his words that mix with theirs, his mute
that's muted by the loud
of ever dust-gilt evenings—

dark planks, bartender,
drinkers shout from sombrero shadows
and blazing doors, sentinel returnings
of glass to table, (kthunk the solid chunk
of heavy-bottomed tympany).

Then bicycle bearings,
cherry forks, wheels and all
unhinge the intimate;
dusk erases guilty muses—
lilting one way, then another,
solid Johnny lands upon the floor.

[D]ía de los muertos

for Clay Blankenship

Lank hair sweet smirk
tipped cup of secrets saluted
into saucerful of smoke
lake night camping in Spanish
bajo las estrellas hablamos
hasta el amanecer
de Lorca y las cosas
que todavía no habían pasado
the half-woven verses left to me
in the sucked riptide of his passing
intimate silk spun from Ariadne
of friendship's tuition
that goes on unthreading
each next seam I go sealing
in my crafty sullen heart.

[J]immy: Notecard #6

I have in my likker decreases
Of shame — Wash my mouth under a spigot
Washes away euclidean squares of pain —
From my stomach pouch I reveal —
Violá! — your losses — gut feelings
Born on the withered bitches that suck
My marsupial brain —
Now to enfold you
In blank arms of the new warrior.

[N]ight Omen: Notecard #27

Sadness flaked off his face
The terrible deep ego
Inflicting gesture and tone —
Words that stumble then spill
In bursts. Glass night
Wounded dry in the lonely locks,
Closure to the hotel room:
Book, penumbra, and Jason
Slip into mute aperture.

[L]ament for the Unknown Dead

Oigo la vida en mi carne
Es su rumor que amo
—*José María Álvarez*

Fortunate for soundbyte's sake
and tremulous with chimney steam
these momentary morning rumors light
up the tremor and down the shakes —
the grip of hand rattles glass
because we are less this day
and grave to the forgetting,
while yet someone else
speaks
cries
screams
and the busyness of regeneration
floods again the electric hollow
of awakening.

[P]ast Mercy: Notecard #20

You weren't there
When the phantom voided
Into grainy photographic
Implosion
So I emptied the bottle myself
At the faded voice
Rain and whiskey
Crackling
In your honor
                    (I swear)

[R]ain Minnow-III

Bone Wood Tone
Drop Let Sof-
       ten

[O]puscule for Dream Sand

Shall I tell you how it dreamed?
Trees made of sand
        tiered   their downfall   billow
topoi of trout clean stream, dale dallied hill,
choked out all by regularity
beneath the form — exact
grainy land. Voices stuttering magma,
soft fire rain, I tripping this eternity through —
animal with legs trap-mauled
iOh tangled undergrowth! iOh conti-
nuity! Persons stick-upended in this
quicksand,
stirring it about-face
when
I left myself arguing with one, becoming one,
his melting words my face cupping,
to let the insolence of dawn
ungrain the silicone divine.

[W]eak-end

Saturday filament
strung out in a sweaty bed,
eternal thread weaving together
a bore-hoard of grimy
lung-heaves—
treasure troves of resurrection
ground into the fine
repeated puncture
of waking half-crocked to the divided
blank of evening
and walking full-tilt
into the dank cotton hours
deathmasked for sleepwalking grimaces
where vicious argonauts plunge down
the watery defile
stripping the body
of all its foci.
Oh Sunday, bone-horned
Sunday, all your cast blame
lowered
groundward
charging.

[V]íspera: Notecard #10

With essy hiss of dawn
And monastery chant behind thin veil of rain
Nudge gorgeous peat boys into real

Damp pages de-fibered upon splinters
Of memory, spineless conscious
shucked of covers

Were that it were you
I'd go looking for a title page
A glorious, embossed binding
But not for Kerry, nor Castilla,
nor moldering pulp of agony

[O]ración vagabunda—From Jaime to His
Belovéd: Notecard #23

Into a mist and hazy sand
Go forth impure food and restless
Inventory of shop-keep items,
Empty from my cavern and desire
Inkpots, exquisite bolts of cloth,
The lacquered taffies,
To leave in full resound of space
The kinder nomad walled with cloth—
His sun-tanned voice draws excellence
From walking, unfettered gazing
Sightless upon another
Body and sense.

[S]tudy of Leavings

Queda quizás el recurso de andar solo,
de vaciar el alma de ternura
y llenarla de hastío e indiferencia,
en este tiempo hostil, propicio al odio.
—Ángel González

Tendrils of hesitation
at my feet in the smoked glass
of accounting offices
then Central Park, full of leaves,
I don't know, but they keep seeking me
repeatedly — damned relatives of the lottery,
claim they always loved me
(round every corner)
and from one season to the next
the alzheimer lines pinnate, untrace
what came before — be-
come memoirs traced
over the broken nose of my belt
and rubber toe-capped sneakers
aged brittle, abused
abusing

gap between humid flesh
and grainy brick —
no account for intimate weathers
or their remains
in my age —
                few left
anyway.

[D]ream Ring

The slight snow, organ-blast train
fill the sense thinly
[freight air]
accompanist trickles a finger
[pianissimo]
y a la vida — bajón, tempranillo —
viene el fulgor verídico
[caricia distraída]
longing the nine o'clock noun
forgoes pleasure
and the blustery winter sunrise

[N]ight Crystals

Walk into new snow
night of mirror, blank page
and rustle of warm chest kernel
where frost fingers breach the numb
into snow-sphere and crystal cackle.
The park wears a bright mantle,
offers jagged soundprints
within pink flush of city
where our pulse scribbles the small hollows:
typocriptic shedding
of muscle memory
into the congress of boughs —
our chorus settles
with a long, creaking sigh.)

Joshua Bridgwater Hamilton

Joshua Hamilton is a Louisville, KY native who migrated to Corpus Christi with his family: spouse and artist Leticia Bajuyo, their daughter, and their rickety but sweet cat, Walnut (RIP). Between Kentucky and Texas, he prowled the halls of the Universidad Complutense de Madrid, hitchhiked in the west of Ireland, kayaked Appalachian rivers, and sweltered in the tropical heat of Panama City, Panamá. Along the way, he has made some amazing friends, lost some, lost himself, followed the pieces to better places, paddled the Colorado River with siblings and spouse, hiked through Peruvian mountains, and gotten to know beautiful people and family all up and down the Philippine islands. He holds degrees in English, Humanities, and Spanish from the University of Louisville and Indiana University. Joshua's field of research focuses on Visual Poetry from the late Franco dictatorship (1960s - 1970s). His first chapbook, *Slow Wind*, was published with Finishing Line Press in 2016.

www.ingramcontent.com/pod-product-compliance
Lightning Source LLC
Chambersburg PA
CBHW021941170626
46807CB00007B/3213